Unlikely Friends

A Story of
Second Chances

Published in Nashville, Tennessee, by Tommy Nelson™, a division of Thomas Nelson, Inc.
Vice President of Children's Books: Laura Minchew; Managing Editor: Beverly Phillips; Art Director: Karen Phillips.

Library of Congress Cataloging-in-Publication Data

Hall, Monica
    Unlikely friends / novelization by Monica Hall ; illustrated by Kevin Burke ; based on a teleplay by Kathleen McGhee-Anderson.
       p.   cm. — (Touched by an angel)
    "Based on the television series created by John Masius."
    Summary: With the guidance of an angel, fifteen-year-old juvenile offender Jason discovers the rewards of working with and helping Kelly, who is in a wheelchair.
    ISBN: 0-8499-5801-6
    [1. Juvenile delinquency—Fiction. 2. Physically handicapped—Fiction. 3. Angels—Fiction.] I. Burke, Kevin, 1957– ill. II. McGhee-Anderson, Kathleen. III. Touched by an angel (Television program). IV. Title. V. Series.
PZ7.H14725At   1999
[Fic]—dc21
                                                   98-31245
                                                    CIP
                                                        AC

Printed in the United States of America

99 00 01 02 03 04 WCV 9 8 7 6 5 4 3 2 1

Unlikely Friends

A Story of Second Chances

A novelization of the television series episode "At Risk"

Novelization by MONICA HALL
Illustrated by KEVIN BURKE
Based on a teleplay by KATHLEEN McGHEE-ANDERSON

MARTHA WILLIAMSON
Executive Producer

Based on the television series created by JOHN MASIUS

Tommy
NELSON

Thomas Nelson, Inc.
Nashville

Growing up in Jason DeLee's neighborhood wasn't fun, or easy, or even safe. And that made him very angry . . . and very scared. Of course, Jason would *never* admit—even to himself— that he was scared. He just worked very hard at showing how tough he was.

If there was trouble to get into, Jason was first in line! Like the time he stole school raffle tickets, or the time the store owner caught him stealing sneakers. But in the past there had always been a way out. This time, however, Jason was caught in a stolen car. And even his mother, who loved him very much, couldn't help him. He didn't know where to turn.

Lena DeLee looked sadly at her son as they sat in the police station. Jason was sure he'd be going home with her just like all the other times. But he was wrong. With tears in her eyes, Lena stood up, touched him gently on the shoulder, and walked to the door. "God help you, baby," she said, "because I don't know how to anymore."

Jason sat alone in the empty room. He knew he'd done the wrong thing by trying to steal a car. Now he didn't know *what* was going to happen; but he knew he wouldn't like it.

Jason was right. He *didn't* like Juvenile Services Camp. He'd already tangled with a scrappy kid named Rey. And the Camp Director, Waters, was one tough dude!

"You do not sit. You do not stand," boomed Waters. "You do not do *anything* until I say so—"

Then, a warm voice floated across the room. "Good afternoon, gentlemen." Every head turned toward the doorway. "My name is Tess. I'm your *other* camp supervisor."

Director Waters looked *very* confused.

"And *this* is Monica," Tess continued serenely. "She is in charge of a new work program. And she needs some volunteers. Strong, smart, hardworking people with a little time on their hands—like you."

Monica beamed at the boys. "Those who volunteer will be helping some very special people. *And* helping themselves, too."

"Oh, sure . . . !" The boys nudged each other and laughed.

"Gentlemen, I'm going to get right to the point," Tess began. "I don't like your lifestyle. *God* doesn't like your lifestyle. And even *you* don't like your lifestyle. But that will change!"

Then, Tess looked right at Jason. "Now . . . any volunteers?"

Thirty minutes later, Jason plopped into a seat on the Juvenile Services Camp bus and opened his favorite car magazine. He had volunteered because there wasn't anything better to do, but he didn't have to *like* it! And he sure didn't have to *smile* about it, like that bus driver, Andrew. That man acted like something great was about to happen!

Jason turned the page. *A Ferrari! Man! A car like that could take you anywhere!*

"But it won't get you where you *really* want to be," said a friendly voice beside him.

Jason stared at Monica with surprise. *Where did she come from? And how did she know what I was thinking?* he wondered.

That was just the *first* surprise. . . .

After the bus came to a stop, Andrew led Jason and the other teenagers into a building that looked like a school. Inside, there were children in wheelchairs. Children in walkers. Children with challenges that these tough street kids had never imagined!

"Oh, man," breathed Jason. "No way!" *They're so little. And so . . . so different.* Just looking at them made him feel scared!

But one by one, the street kids from Juvenile Camp were partnered with the children in the class. And for Jason . . . there was Kelly.

He stared at the frail little girl slumped in her wheelchair. "What's wrong with her?" he whispered.

"Kelly was born with cerebral palsy," Monica answered softly. "She came into this world unable to walk, or talk, or hold her head up. She has to work very hard to do things that *you* take for granted."

For the first week, Jason couldn't even get Kelly to *look* at him! But one day, as he passed the time daydreaming over his car magazine, a small hand crept over and tugged at his sleeve.

"She's trying to get your attention," said Monica. "I think she likes that Ferrari as much as you do." And that gave Jason an idea. . . .

He tore out the page and taped it to her wheelchair. "Okay, Kelly, if you like cars, let's go for a ride!—Va-room . . . Va-room!"

Jason and Kelly zigged and zagged around the classroom very fast. For the first time since he'd volunteered, Jason felt like he was being useful. And he was having fun . . . until Andrew stepped in front of them.

"This isn't a game, Jason," Andrew said sternly. "You could hurt Kelly."

"Well, I gotta go to the restroom," Jason mumbled angrily. He hadn't meant any harm.

Andrew sighed. "Okay. Two minutes."

Inside the tiny restroom, Jason puffed on a stolen cigarette, wishing he were out of here.

"Running away isn't the answer, Jason."

Quickly dropping the cigarette, Jason whirled around. There stood Monica! "You can't come in here," he said. "This is the men's room!"

"You'd be surprised where my work takes me," she smiled. "And where *your* work with Kelly could take *you,* if you let it."

Jason sighed. "I can't help her. She's too messed up."

"People say that about you, too," Monica said gently. "They say that *you're* a waste of time."

That gave Jason a lot to think about. How many times had he wished someone would give him a chance? Maybe this *was* his chance to do something right.

He went back to the classroom.

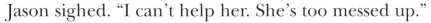

Jason put his hands on each side of Kelly's face, and lifted her head. "Look at me, Kelly. If you don't look at me, you won't be able to see how ugly I am." And then he made a silly face.

As Kelly's head drooped back down, Jason heard a tiny little sound. "Did you laugh? Did I hear a laugh?"

He was so excited, he forgot all about acting tough. He reached out and hugged Kelly. Suddenly, she began to cough . . . harder and harder.

Kelly's mother rushed over. "She's choking!" she said. "I smell smoke on your clothes, Jason. Kelly is allergic to cigarette smoke!"

Andrew was angry, too. "You know smoking is against the rules, Jason. These are children with disabilities. Either use your head, or don't come back here!"

Jason was still upset the next day. All his life he'd been getting into trouble, and now when he thought he was helping, he was still getting into trouble!

Tess understood, but her voice was stern as she explained, "You have to think about what you do, Jason. Use your mind!" Then she smiled. "You have a very good one, you know."

Jason looked so surprised, Tess couldn't help laughing. "What? Nobody ever told you that before? Well, you do. God gave you a very good mind. Of course, you've made mistakes. We all do. But if you can honestly say you are sorry and sincerely try to do better, then I'll give you another chance."

After talking with Andrew, even Kelly's mother, Anita, was willing to let Jason try again. "You were so busy watching Jason," said Andrew, "you didn't see what happened with Kelly."

Anita didn't understand. "What happened?"

Andrew smiled. "She laughed," he said.

"She laughed? Well . . ." said Anita, "Jason might be good for Kelly after all."

Jason worked very hard with Kelly over the next few weeks. He was very proud of Kelly, and himself. He'd even recorded his name on a tape player and showed her how to push the button. *Ja-son* the machine played back. *Ja-son.*

"Here, Kelly, you try it. Push this button and you can call me anytime you want." But her hand wouldn't do what she wanted. "Never mind, little girl," Jason said gently. "Someday you'll be able to do it."

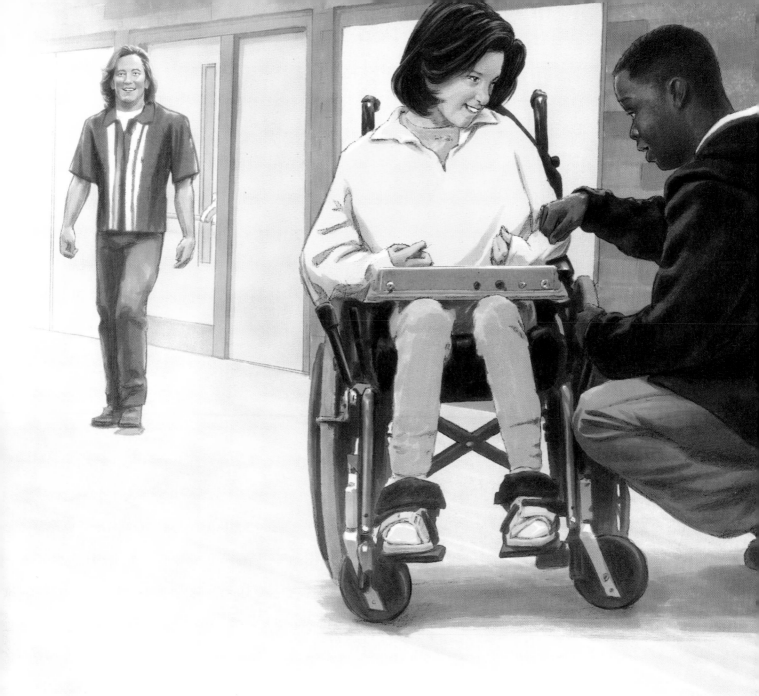

"You know, Jason, you're really good at this." Jason looked up in surprise at a smiling Andrew. "I mean it," Andrew said. "You ought to think about going to school so you can do this for a living."

Jason stared as Andrew walked away. Could he really have a *future*? Could he really *change* that much?

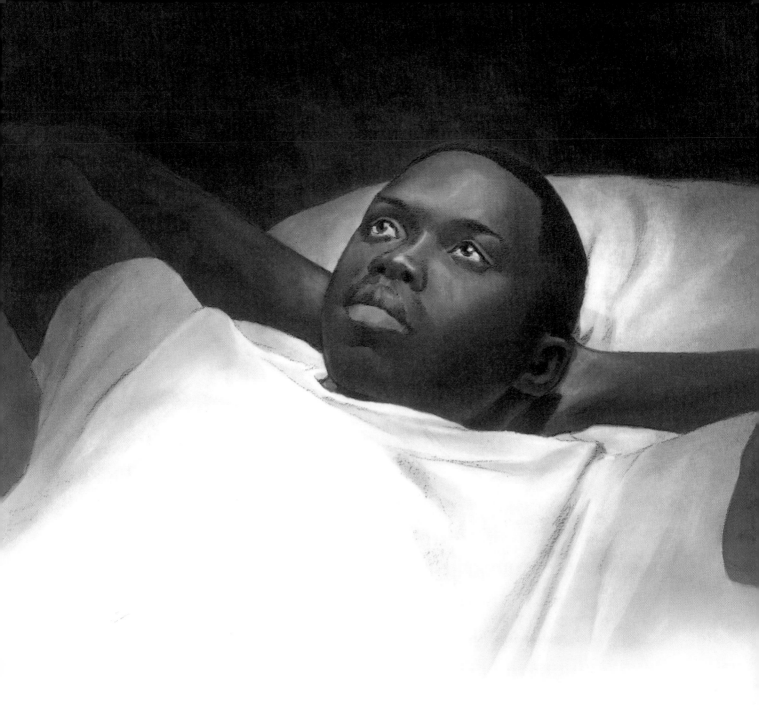

Over the next few weeks, the other boys from the camp saw how hard Jason was working, and how much Kelly mattered to him. They made fun of him for thinking he could make a difference or amount to anything.

In bed, one night, Jason just stared into the dark, his thoughts racing. *Andrew said I'm doing well, but how could anything I do matter? The guys are right. I don't really have a future.* Jason told himself that the only way out was to get away. He began to make plans.

The next day, inside the car showroom, Jason watched from his hiding place as the last salesman locked the door and left. He was alone with the cars he loved.

He slipped into the soft leather seat of the gleaming red Ferrari. Then, as he reached out with the key he had taken from the salesman's desk, a quiet voice broke the silence. "You haven't thought this through, have you?"

Jason jumped. Standing right beside the car—where she hadn't been a second ago—was Monica!

"You'd like to take the easy way out and just drive out of here," she continued, "but the easy way isn't always the right way. I thought you'd learned that the way to reach a goal is to work for it, not run from it."

Jason shrugged. "I got tired of working. What's the point?"

"Oh, Jason!" exclaimed Monica. "God made you to *live* in this world—to make it *better*. And you know what? You've done that with Kelly. God is very proud of you."

What?! Jason looked up, and his eyes grew very big.

"I'm an angel, Jason," Monica said gently. "And God made *me* for a special purpose, too . . . to tell you that He *loves* you.

"He's always with you, Jason," Monica continued. "And the fastest car can't outrun Him. Wherever you go, He'll be there, waiting with the answer. Miracles do happen."

"But people like me don't get miracles," Jason said.

Monica touched his shoulder lightly. "You've already been given one. Her name is Kelly."

Kelly sat still as a mouse in her wheelchair. She wouldn't look at anyone, or anything. The one face—the one voice— that she wanted most of all wasn't there.

Jason's mother, had come to the school hoping to find her runaway boy. "My son worked here?" she asked. "He was helping this little girl?" Her worried eyes began to shine with pride.

Just then, Jason burst in. "All my life, I just wanted to get in a car and go. But when I had the chance . . ." his voice shook, "I realized the only place I wanted to be was *here*."

Tears filled Jason's eyes as he
looked at Kelly. "Because I missed
Kelly and I missed helping her." He
took his mother's hand. "I was finally
doing something good, something
that would make you proud of me,
and I wanted to share it with you."

Jason knelt beside the silent little
girl. "Kelly? Kel?"

Very slowly, Kelly lifted her head up—eyes bright—and beamed at Jason. Then she reached out a shaky hand and pushed the button on the tape player. Again and again . . . *Ja-son. Ja-son. Ja-son.* It was a song, a celebration!

Together, with their heads held high, Kelly and Jason smiled.

Maybe Andrew was right, thought Jason. *Maybe I do have a future. Maybe I can make a difference.*
For Kelly, he already had.